SO-BCW-198

MOP, MOP, MOP!

Written by Wiley Blevins
Illustrated by Jessica Wolk-Stanley

SCHOLASTIC INC.

New York Toronto London Auckland Sydney
Mexico City New Delhi Hong Kong Buenos Aires

ISBN 0-439-31964-1

Copyright © 2000 by Scholastic Inc. All rights reserved. Published by Scholastic Inc. Portions previously published in SCHOLASTIC DECODABLE READERS. SCHOLASTIC, SCHOLASTIC PHONICS READY READERS, and associated logos are trademarks and/or registered trademarks of Scholastic Inc.

12 11 10 9 8 7 6 5 4 3 2   1 2 3 4 5 6/0
Printed in the U.S.A.   08

Mop, mop, mop.

Mom mops a lot.

Hop, hop, hop.

Tom hops a lot.

Mop, mop, mop.

Mom and Tom mop a lot!

Vowel /o/o

hop
hops
lot
Mom
mop
mops
Tom